Titles in Dark Reads:

Blood Moon
Barbara Catchpole

Doctor Jekyll and Little Miss Hyde
Tony Lee

Red Handed
Ann Evans

Ringtone
Tommy Donbavand

Ship of the Dead
Alex Woolf

Straw Men
Ann Evans

The Black-Eyed Girl
Tim Collins

The Girl in the Wall
Tommy Donbavand

Badger Publishing Limited, Oldmedow Road, Hardwick Industrial Estate, King's Lynn PE30 4JJ
Telephone: 01438 791037

www.badgerlearning.co.uk

BARBARA CATCHPOLE

Badger
L E A R N I N G

Blood Moon ISBN 978-1-78464-089-7

Publisher: Susan Ross
Senior Editor: Danny Pearson
Publishing Assistant: Claire Morgan
Copyeditor: Cheryl Lanyon
Designer: Bigtop Design Ltd
Illustrator: Nigel Dobbyn

2 4 6 8 10 9 7 5 3

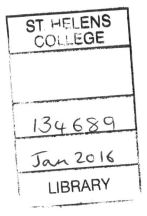

CHAPTER 1

NOTEBOOK

My name is Matt Blake. I was a plainclothes policeman. I solved crime in the busy city of London.

I only worked on really bad crime. Often my days were full of murder and blood. Lee was my partner and my mate. He always had my back.

After work Lee and I went to the gym together. Sometimes we went to clubs together.

Lee wasn't anything special but I was really fit!

Now everything is different, all because of my last case. This is my police notebook. Read about it!

"Matt, Matt," Lee grabbed his keys and ran for the car.

"Holy Moly!" (He was always saying crazy stuff like that.)

"Someone has stolen a pack of wolves from London Zoo! Six wolves!"

That *was* strange.

CHAPTER 2
HOSPITAL

The keeper was very upset. "Don't shoot them!" he said.

"Stay calm, sir," I said.

"An adult wolf weighs forty-five kilograms. They eat ten kilograms of bloody meat a day! They can rip your throat out!" he said.

I went to phone our snipers but my phone went off. It was Cut–'em-up Susie, saying to come quick. She looks after our dead bodies.

It's nothing to do with the case, but I was going to ask Susie out. She's clever and pretty and… Anyway! She told us to meet her at the hospital.

*

"It's a homeless guy. They found him outside the hospital!" Susie said. "But just look at this… I've never seen anything like it!"

A sheet was covering the body. She lifted it off. It was horrible!

The man was a monster. It looked like he was part wolf. His hands were wolf claws! He had yellow fangs! A strong hairy tail hung down below the steel table.

I thought I heard a wolf howl somewhere in the hospital.

Lee looked at me and we said it together,

"Holy Moly!"

*

We talked to the homeless guys under
the bridge near the hospital.

We showed them the dead wolfman's photo.

"The Doc took him – the Doc from the
hospital! He takes them all!" one man cried.

CHAPTER 3
THE WOLVES

The hospital! That's where Susie was!

"Run, Lee, run! Out of our way! Armed police!"

I knew I had heard wolves! We burst into the lab next to Susie's. The wolves were in a big cage in the corner. All except one, who was in a big glass tank. Next to the wolf, tied up, was Susie.

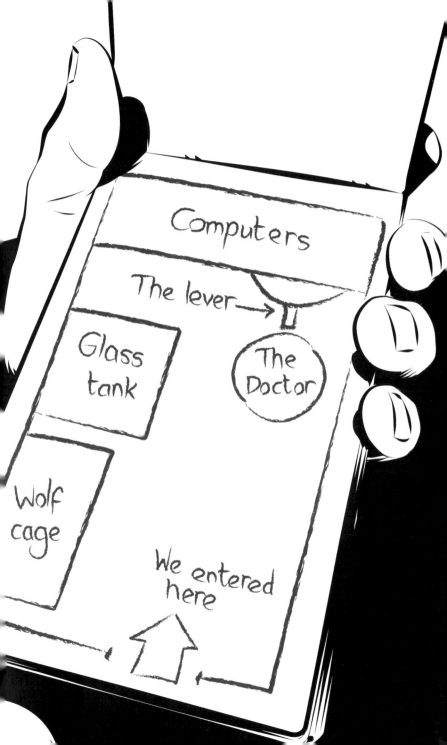

Susie screamed. The wolves howled.
I could hear mad, mad laughter.

A voice said, "When I pull the lever, the
girl will be half wolf! I shall be rich! Rich,
I tell you!"

He was only a little weedy bloke – a real
mad doctor. We had to stop him!

Lee struggled with the doctor.

I tried to get into the tank. The glass door was locked. I hit the door with a chair and it smashed.

The pieces fell to the floor.

CHAPTER 4
OUT COLD

"Thank you! Thank you!" Susie was free.

I was still in the tank when the doctor got away from Lee. He pulled the lever and a shock ran through me. I couldn't move.

I saw lights and my head really hurt.

"Matt!" Lee yelled, "No! No!"

*

"Are you OK, mate?"

Yes, I was OK. No fangs, no claws. No tail!

"But how…?" I began.

Lee grinned. "The team arrived and grabbed the doctor. You were out cold. But I think we stopped his experiment in time."

*

At home I sat and ate a steak, red and raw, dripping with blood. It tasted great! I drove back to the zoo to set my pack free.

The moon was full and red – a blood moon.

I wanted to run with the wolves and howl at the red moon. We could hunt together.

STORY FACTS

WOLVES

Real wolves live in packs. They can eat up to a fifth of their body weight. The heaviest wolf ever was 80 kilograms! Each pack has a pair of 'boss wolves' who eat first. In some countries, such as Italy, there are real packs of wild wolves living quite near humans.

There are lots of wolves in books. Werewolves are half man and half wolf. The person turns into a wolf at full moon. There are also stories about people who 'shapeshift' into a wolf.

QUESTIONS

Where did Lee and Matt go after work?
(page 6)

How many wolves had been stolen from London Zoo?
(page 8)

Who called Matt whilst he was at the zoo?
(page 10)

What Did Matt eat?
(page 28)

How much did the heaviest wolf ever weigh?
(page 30)

What happens to a werewolf at full moon?
(page 30)

Barbara Catchpole used to be a teacher. She has three grown-up sons and a grandson (hello Finlay!). She has written lots of books for teenagers.

Nigel Dobbyn has been illustrating books and comics for over 25 years. He has worked for titles such as *2000AD*, *Sonic the Comic*, *Classical Comics* and *The Beano*.